ROBERT STARLING

FERGAL MEETS FERN

ANDERSEN PRESS

This is Fergal.

And this is Fergal
with his mum
and dad.

He's a happy little chap.

Or he was, until
Mum and Dad
brought home
the egg.

It didn't do much at first.

Everyone just watched it and waited.

TAP
TAP TAP

And then one day, it hatched!

Inside the egg was Fergal's new baby sister, Fern.

Suddenly, the house was full of visitors coming to meet Fern and give her presents.

Fergal was starting to feel a bit funny until Nan-dragon brought a present for him too. Tickets for the flying show!

But Fergal's good mood didn't last long.
From bedtime to playtime Fern spoiled everything.

She played with
his toys. It made
Fergal feel **fiery**,
but he kept it
to himself.

She cried in the car.
It made Fergal feel
really fiery,
but he kept it
to himself.

WAAAAAA!

Then, on the day of
the flying show, Fern got sick.
"I'm sorry darling," said Mum,
"but Dad needs to get Fern's
medicine, so he can't take you
to the flying show.
We'll all go another time."

As they went to
buy the medicine,
Fergal felt the fiery feeling building up inside him.

No one noticed him. No one ever noticed him. He decided to **run away**.

When Dad realised
Fergal had gone he
was really worried.

Everyone helped to look,

but no one
could spot him.

It was Dad who finally found Fergal.

"I was so worried," he said, wiping away Fergal's tears. "Why would you run away?" "I didn't think you'd care," gulped Fergal, "now you've got Fern."

"Why didn't you tell me how you were feeling?" asked Dad. "Let's get some fresh air."

Fergal told Dad that sometimes Fern made him feel fiery. He knew it was wrong, so he kept the feeling secret.

"Feelings aren't right or wrong," said Dad.
"But keep them bottled up inside and they can hurt you."

Fergal said he felt jealous because Fern got everyone's love. "Babies need a special kind of love, because they're so new and little," said Dad.

little artist

"It was the same when you were small. Take a look."

It was Fergal's baby book! Inside he could see Mum and Dad doing all those baby things with him.

Later, Fergal had another feeling to tell
Dad about: he felt worried because
everything was so different now.

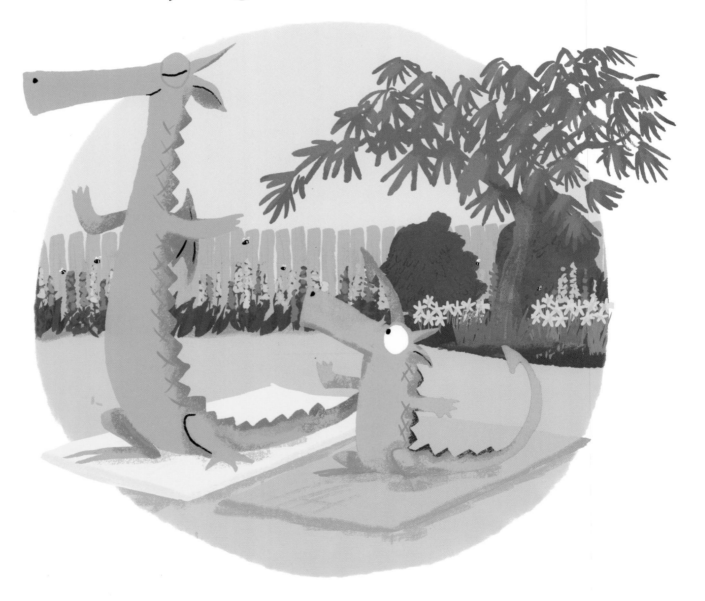

"One big thing that is different is you, Fergal," said Dad.
"I'm not different!" said Fergal.

"Yes, you are," said Dad.
"You're a big brother now."

Fergal thought about it.
He liked the sound of that.

Finally Fergal told Dad about feeling sad
because everyone always looked at Fern.

"Have you ever noticed who Fern always looks at?"
asked Dad. Fergal didn't know. "She looks at you, Fergal.
When she does, what do you think she sees?"

Fergal thought. He was always fiery or worried or sad or jealous when Fern was around.

"I guess she sees... a grumpy big brother."

So Fergal decided
to make a change.

And it turned out
Mum and Dad
were so busy,

WOOOOOSH!!!

CLICK!

that a big
brother had a
really important
job to do.

Something that would make
sure Fern remembered exactly
how Fergal felt about her.
Because...